The Magic Potions Shop

The Lightning Pup

By Abie Longstaff & Lauren Beard:

The Fairytale Hairdresser and Rapunzel

The Fairytale Hairdresser and Cinderella

The Fairytale Hairdresser and Sleeping Beauty

The Fairytale Hairdresser and Snow White

The Fairytale Hairdresser and Father Christmas

The Fairytale Hairdresser and the Little Mermaid

The Fairytale Hairdresser and the Sugar Plum Fairy

The Fairytale Hairdresser and Beauty and the Beast

The Magic Potions Shop: The Young Apprentice

The Magic Potions Shop: The River Horse

The Magic Potions Shop: The Blizzard Bear

The Magic Potions Shop

The Lightning Pup

Abie Longstaff & Lauren Beard

RED FOX

RED FOX

UK I USA I Canada I Ireland I Australia
India I New Zealand I South Africa

Red Fox is part of the Penguin Random House group of companies
whose addresses can be found at global.penguinrandomhouse.com.

www.penguin.co.uk
www.puffin.co.uk
www.ladybird.co.uk

Penguin
Random House
UK

First published 2016

001

Text copyright © Abie Longstaff, 2016
Illustrations copyright © Lauren Beard and Penguin Random House Children's
UK, 2016

The moral right of the author and illustrator has been asserted

Set in Palatino Regular 16/23pt
Printed in Great Britain by Clays Ltd, St Ives plc

A CIP catalogue record for this book is available from the British Library

ISBN: 978–1–782–95192–6

All correspondence to:
Red Fox
Penguin Random House Children's
80 Strand, London WC2R 0RL

For Archie and Jackson
– A.L.

Chapter One

It was lunch time in the Potions
Shop and Tibben's tummy was
growling. He rubbed it and tried
to block all thoughts of delicious
Honey Berries from his mind. This
was no time for eating! There was
far too much to do! The pixie shook
his head and concentrated on the
Mage Stone in his hand.

For the past three days, Tibben
had been trying to make

Transformation Gel.

If he got it right, the gel was supposed to change the **Mage Stone** into something else. But *Transformation Gel* was a very difficult potion. Not only did Tibben have to make exactly the right mixture, but he had to focus hard and imagine the object the stone was supposed to change into. So far Tibben hadn't managed to change the stone into anything at all, and it just lay in his hand, round and grey.

Tibben sighed. He was fed up. "I can't do it, Grandpa."

Grandpa was the Potions Master – it was his job to train Tibben,

and he was sure Tibben was
ready for the challenge of making
Transformation Gel.

"Come on, my boy," he said.
"Have another go."

"I'll try later," said Tibben. "I
need to help with the customers."

Wizz was out gathering plants
and seeds for potions, so there
was only Grandpa serving behind
the counter. As usual, there was
an enormous queue of creatures
waiting to be served. They had
come from all over the Kingdom
of Arthwen to find the largest tree

in Steadysong Forest; the tree that
was the home of the Potions Shop.

"I can manage," called Grandpa
as he made a barrel of *Waterskate
Powder* for a Silver Squirrel's
birthday party. "Why don't you try
changing the stone into a teacup?"

Tibben sighed again. He looked

longingly at Grandpa's cloak, which was covered in **Glints**, the magical sign of potions skill. Tibben fingered the green fabric of his own cloak. So far he had three **Glints**: *Crystal*, *Opal* and *Pearl*. He rubbed their jagged edges and bumped his finger across each facet. It felt like ages since he had earned a **Glint**: the last time was when he and Wizz had visited the Frozen

Tundra to help
Karhu, the
Blizzard Bear.
Tibben was
desperate to
make it to
Ruby level.
Then there
would only be
Diamond to get
before he could take
the Master's Challenge and become
a Potions Master, just like Grandpa!

Tibben watched Grandpa
bending over his **Mage Nut** bowl.
He was nearly 100 years old now.
Very soon he would be retiring
to the Vale of Years and then . . .

then Tibben would have to take over as Potions Master. Tibben shivered at the thought. He wasn't ready. He wasn't anywhere near ready.

Tibben shook his head and opened a heavy book with a red leather cover. On the front, in bumpy gold lettering, were the words *The Book of Potions*. This was the potions training manual. It held recipes for all the different

potions, creams, ointments, drams, remedies and powders that Tibben needed to learn. He turned to the right page:

8

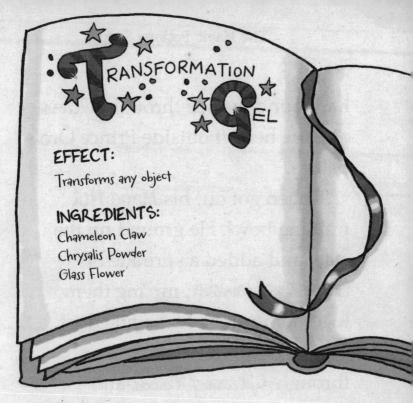

EFFECT:
Transforms any object

INGREDIENTS:
Chameleon Claw
Chrysalis Powder
Glass Flower

All the ingredients were very
rare.

Chameleon Claw had to
be exchanged with the Rainbow
Chameleons on Blue Mountain.
Chrysalis Powder came from
abandoned butterfly houses in
Moonlight Meadow, and Wizz

had found the see-through *Glass Flower* herself outside Prince Oro's palace.

Tibben got out his **Mage Nut** training bowl. He ground up the claw and added a sprinkle of *Chrysalis Powder*, mixing them together until he had a fine dust. Then, gently, he lifted the see-through *Glass Flower* and squeezed the liquid from its stem. The dust dissolved with a fizz, and the mixture was instantly clear.

Tibben screwed up his face. He was determined to get it right this time. He looked at the stone and pictured a teacup in his mind, trying to imagine the handle, the

smooth china surface, the shape
of the cup. He concentrated really
hard and, to his amazement, the
Mage Stone began to turn white
and a handle started to appear!

"It's working!" he laughed. But
at that very moment Wizz flung
open the door of
the Potions
Shop.

"Wizz
find Spider
Grass!" she
announced in
excitement.

"That's wonderful, Wizz!"
Grandpa cried. "Spider Grass is
a very rare plant indeed!"

Suddenly all Tibben could think about were spiders. Desperately he tried to force his mind back onto the teacup. But it was too late. In despair he watched as his **Mage Stone** carried on changing into a most peculiar creature.

It was white . . .

It was round . . .

It had a handle . . .

. . . and eight hairy spider legs.

Tibben had invented a Teacup Spider. The creature opened its beady eyes and began to run around the shop. Customers called out in amazement as it bumped into jars and bottles and tried to climb the shelves.

"Wizz!" Tibben snapped. "You ruined my transformation!"

"No, Tibben," said Grandpa. "You have to learn to focus better."

Tibben scowled and looked up. The Teacup Spider had found a lovely dark space under a shelf and was starting to build a little ceramic web . . . in the shape of a teapot.

Chapter Two

"Sorry wooz." Wizz appeared at Tibben's side with a plate of **Honey Berries** for him.

"Oh, Wizz. It wasn't really your fault," said Tibben. "I'm sorry I snapped at you." He gobbled a handful of berries. "Mmmm." He smiled as the warm honey liquid slipped down his throat and into his tummy.

"Try weez?" Wizz asked.

"Yes, I'm trying again," said
Tibben. "What about you?" He
felt like he hadn't seen his friend
for days. She was off gathering
ingredients all the time now.

"Wizz good!" Her white fluffy
face spread into a huge grin as she
showed him her Gathering Diary.
filled with drawings and bits of
leaves and seeds.

"Yes, Wizz is doing very well," came Grandpa's deep voice from the wooden counter of the Potions Shop. "She's found some wonderful plants recently."

"Oh." Tibben looked down. It really was good that Wizz was doing so well, he told himself. Really good.

All of a sudden Wizz froze. Her nose twitched and her whiskers went taut.

"What is it?" said Tibben.

"Can you sense something, Wizz?" asked Grandpa.

Wizz didn't answer. Her nose was turned up and she was sniffing the air.

Grandpa and Tibben looked at one another, puzzled.

"Bug bug coming," said Wizz.

"What do you mean, Wizz?" asked Tibben.

"Bug bug coming," Wizz repeated.

Tibben looked at Grandpa, and Grandpa looked at Wizz.

Just then the bluebell of the Potions Shop jangled, and into the shop crawled a little Mud Bug with a broken shell.

"Wow!" Tibben's eyes widened. "How did you know he was coming, Wizz?"

Wizz just shrugged.

"Oh, Wizz!" cried Grandpa, clapping his hands together. "Do you know what you can do?!"

"Weez?"

"You can sense creatures now! Not just plants and flowers but real creatures!"

Wizz grinned.

"This is wonderful!" Grandpa continued. "I've never even heard

19

of a Gatherer who can do that!"
He lifted Wizz by her paws and
swung her around the shop.

"Wheee!" Wizz squealed.
"That's amazing, Wizz," Tibben
said quietly.

"It's fantastic!" cried Grandpa. "It's brilliant! Wizz, you are truly gifted."

Wizz grinned even wider.

"Right!" said Grandpa, grabbing a basket. "We must go and practise straight away! Tibben," he called over his shoulder, "watch the shop, please!"

And, just like that, Grandpa and Wizz were gone. Tibben looked at the Mud Bug and shrugged. The Mud Bug looked at Tibben and raised his antennae.

Chapter Three

Tibben carefully mixed **Iron Cream** and painted it on the Mud Bug's broken shell. The bug lifted his antennae in thanks and Tibben waved goodbye.

The bug was the last of the day's customers and now Tibben was all alone in the shop. It was just him . . . and his stone. On and on he worked, trying to get the *Transformation Gel* just right.

Wizz and Grandpa had been gone for ages! *They must be working hard*, thought Tibben. He sighed. It was good that Wizz was doing so well, he told himself for the millionth time. And it was good that Grandpa was so impressed with her.

"Ohhh." Tibben put his head in his hands. If only he could get the gel right! Then Grandpa would be impressed with him too.

Ding-dong! went the bluebell of the Potions Shop. There was a burst of bright light; and a puppy bounded into the shop.

He had bright purple fur, with a zigzag of white down his nose.

"Padge!" cried Tibben. He was so happy to see a friend, he ran over and hugged the dog.

"Woof!" Padge barked in excitement. Padge was a Lightning Pup. He was one of King Krono's messenger dogs, famed throughout the land for their speed and loyalty. Tucked into his collar was a rolled-up scroll. It read:

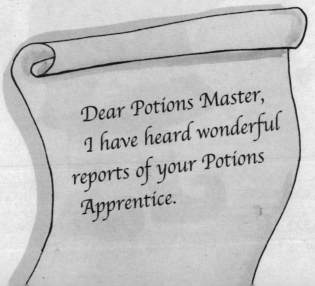

Dear Potions Master,
I have heard wonderful reports of your Potions Apprentice.

"That's me!" cried Tibben in excitement.

I hear he fixed the water in Lake Sapphire and the darkness in the Frozen Tundra.

"Yes I did!" Tibben told Padge.

I would like to invite him to the palace today. I need his help with a problem.
Yours,
Prince Oro

"Wow!" breathed Tibben. "Prince Oro!" He couldn't believe it: Prince Oro lived in such a grand palace – he was famous! And he wanted to meet Tibben!

Tibben grinned. He was going to meet the prince! He'd get to see the inside of the palace and he and Wizz— Wait. He stopped. No; not Wizz.

The invitation was just for him, the Potions Apprentice. For a moment he felt a little bit sad; Wizz had helped him clean the water in Lake Sapphire. She had helped him put the Ice Star back into the sky above the Frozen Tundra.

Then he remembered that, recently, Wizz hadn't been quite so helpful. She was busy these days with her Gathering. It was all she talked about! She had even ruined his *Transformation Gel* earlier just because of *Spider Grass*. Tibben frowned. Grandpa was so proud of Wizz. It was like they had a little club of their own: they kept going off together to pick plants, leaving him behind.

Tibben nodded; Wizz was doing well, he told himself. She didn't need to go to the palace.

Tibben wrote a note to Grandpa and Wizz to tell them he'd be back later. He left the note on the wooden counter and, at the last moment, grabbed

Grandpa

Grandpa's old stone and a vial of *Transformation Gel*.

"Let's go!" he cried, and the puppy barked in answer.

Then he closed the door of the Potions Shop behind him and set off north through Steadysong Forest towards Prince Oro's palace, the Lightning Pup leading the way.

Chapter Four

"Slow down!" Tibben called out to the Lightning Pup. Padge was so fast! As he ran, his paws sparked and crackled with light like sparklers. One moment he was right in front of Tibben, then there was a bright flash and – crack! – the puppy shot ahead.

Tibben rushed to catch up. He couldn't wait to get to the palace. His mind was filled with all the wonderful things he'd see. Prince Oro was rich and powerful; they called him the Golden Prince. His father was King Krono and the prince had a whole palace to himself just outside Steadysong Forest. He hardly ever came out – even Grandpa had never met him. Tibben hugged himself and smiled; the Potions Apprentice would get to meet the prince even before the Potions Master! He giggled and skipped through the forest.

Spring was coming! Tibben could feel it in the air: the flowers were just beginning to open and the grass was growing back. *But never mind that*, he told himself, *there'll be lots of exciting things at the palace.*

Tibben passed right by a 𝕾𝖎𝖑𝖊𝖓𝖙 𝕭𝖆𝖗𝖐 𝕿𝖗𝖊𝖊, with its familiar hollow trunk. From inside he heard a frantic rustling. For a moment he almost stopped; but no, he had to keep going. It was probably nothing – maybe just a creature waking up after winter.

"Let's hurry," said Tibben to the Lightning Pup. He was so excited about seeing the prince.

On they went, right to the edge of

Steadysong Forest. Tibben shivered.
The air didn't feel so fresh and
spring-like now. It was misty and
heavy. He shook his head crossly;
surely he was nearly there? It felt
like he had walked for ages!

Soon they came to the palace
gates.

They shone golden in the hazy light and Tibben touched the fancy markings. He pushed them open and followed Padge down the path towards the palace.

It was so very smart! All around him were beautiful golden sculptures of dragons and fairies and mermaids and centaurs.

Then, as the path turned, he saw the palace entrance. Golden stairs wound their way right up to an enormous golden door, which was glowing in the evening light. Tibben took a deep breath. He pressed the doorbell and heard the sound of a trumpet. He was here! He was actually here!

The heavy door opened with a creak and Tibben was met by a tall butler wearing a fancy wig and a smart uniform.

"Um . . . hello," said Tibben. "I'm here to see Prince Oro."

"Yes, sir," said the butler, and he waved Tibben in.

Tibben tiptoed behind Padge
down a long corridor covered in thick
soft carpet. On the walls were large
paintings and detailed tapestries.

He could hear music ahead, and as he turned a corner he saw the great hall before him. There, a dance troupe was performing to music, while trapeze artists swung across the ceiling.

On a big sofa lay a man, being fed chocolates by his chef. The man sat up when he saw Tibben. It was Oro, the Golden Prince!

"Hey, come in," he drawled. He was wearing a velvet dressing gown and sparkly red shoes that curled up at the toes. The crown on his head was sitting crookedly, as if it was about to fall off. Around his neck hung lots of golden chains and sparkly jewels. Padge settled down beside him, yawning.

40

"Hello . . . um, your majesty," said Tibben, bowing.

The prince laughed and came over to Tibben, then clapped him on the back. "So you're the famous Potions Apprentice, eh?"

Tibben blushed bright pink. "Yes," he said proudly.

"That's cool," said the prince and Tibben grinned. Oro clapped his hands and Tibben saw his jewelled rings shining in the light.

"Go!" shouted the prince. "All

of you. And Chef: we'll want cake.
Three tiers please."

"Yes, your highness." The chef
bowed.

Tibben shivered.

"Come and sit by the fire,"
Oro said, leading him to the sofa.

"So," he went on, "I hear
you cleaned the water in Lake
Sapphire."

"Yes."

"And you put the Ice Star back
in the sky!"

Tibben smiled.

"Wow. Cool. You must be really
powerful, I guess, to be able to do
that by yourself!"

"Ah . . ." Tibben was about to

say that Wizz had helped, but the prince was staring at him, a look of wonder on his face, so he shut his mouth and just nodded. He pulled his cloak around him for warmth and his **Glints** sparkled in the firelight.

"**Glints!**" said Oro. "Hey, I've heard of those. Never seen one though."

Shyly Tibben lifted the edge of his cloak to show Oro. Each **Glint** was different, glowing in its own special way. "I'm going to get another one soon," said Tibben suddenly. "**Ruby**!"

"When?"

"Oh. I just have to make a potion." Tibben waved his hand airily. "Any day now, really."

The prince nodded and his crown nearly fell off. "Whoops!" he said. "Actually that's what I wanted to talk to you about."

"What?"

"My crown," said the prince. "It keeps slipping off. I was hoping you could make something to fix it in place . . ."

For an instant Tibben was really disappointed. Was this the big

problem Prince Oro had called
him to the palace for? His crown
falling off?

"Then," Oro continued, "let's
have dinner together."

Tibben smiled.

"The cake is
ready, your
highness,"
said the chef,
balancing
a three-tiered
cream cake on
a tray.

"Mmm,
delicious!" said
Tibben. Yes.
It was going

to be a great evening here. It didn't matter what problem the prince had.

Chapter Five

Tibben set up his **Mage Nut** bowl by the fire in the great hall, ready to make the *Sticking Potion*.

Oro leaned forward to watch. "How do you make it?" he asked.

"I use this recipe." Tibben opened *The Book of Potions* and pointed to:

Sticking POTION

EFFECT: Sticks anything to anything

INGREDIENTS:
Gumspider Web
Red Clay
Troll Slime

"Wizz found the *Gumspider Web* in Steadysong Forest and the **Red Clay** at the bottom of Bubble River."

"Wizz? Who's Wizz?"

"Oh, she's my friend. She's a Gatherer," Tibben said proudly.

"Can she make potions too?" asked the prince.

"No," said Tibben.

The prince sniffed dismissively. He picked up *The Book of Potions* and began turning the pages. Tibben felt a shiver of cold pass through his body.

"Now I squeeze the *Troll Slime* and the **Red Clay** into the bowl and mix it with the web." Tibben

stirred the mixture until it became
a gloopy mass. Big bubbles of air
rose and popped on the surface.
He dipped his spoon in to catch a
tiny bit of potion, spread it onto
Oro's crown and put the crown
back on the Golden Prince's head.

"There you go!" he said, but
the prince didn't seem to notice.
He was too busy flicking through
The Book of Potions. Tibben
frowned.

"There's nothing here for gold,"
said the prince crossly. He folded
his arms and looked sulky for a
moment. Then he sat up. "Hey,
Tibben, how would you make
gold?" he asked.

"Gold?"

"Yeah."

"Um . . . I don't think there's anything in the book about making gold." Tibben looked at the prince. "Why do you want to make gold?"

"I just like gold things." Oro shrugged. "Take this rug." He nudged it with his toe. "Wouldn't it be cool if it were gold?"

"Well," said Tibben, "it wouldn't be warm and soft then."

"Yes," said Oro, "but it would be shiny!"

Tibben looked at the glowing fire and nodded slowly. It would be amazing to see the rug shine! Suddenly he sat up and fumbled in his bag. "Yes!" he cried. "I thought I'd brought it!"

"What's that?"

Tibben held up the vial of *Transformation Gel*. "This might be a way to make something gold!" he said in excitement.

Prince Oro grinned. "Wow!" he said. "That is sooo cool! Do you think you can do it?" He looked at Tibben in pure admiration.

Tibben nodded. "I think so, and . . . and if I get it right I should get another Glint!"

Tibben lifted the vial of *Transformation Gel* and carefully painted it on the rug. Then he sat back and focused on gold. It wasn't hard, actually; here in the palace the image of gold was easy to summon. Tibben thought of the golden gates he had seen, the golden door and the yellow flames sparkling and dancing . . .

"You did it!" cried Oro loudly.

Tibben opened his eyes. There, where the soft rug had been, was now a square of glittering gold!

"I love it!" Prince Oro lay down on the hard golden surface. "I love it so much!"

Tibben looked down at his cloak. Wait . . . where was the Glint?

"That's not fair," he said crossly.

"I was supposed to get a **Glint**!"

"A **Glint**? Who cares about
a **Glint** now?" said Oro. "We
have gold!!" His eyes grew wide.
"You are amazing!" he cried,
swinging Tibben round and round.
"Amazing! I'm going to give
you everything you
want. If you could
just stay here with
me a while

and make a few more things golden
– OK?" He looked at Tibben with
pleading eyes.

Tibben smiled. *I guess I could
stay for a bit*, he thought to himself,
and he pushed the Glint out of his
mind.

"The cake! The cake! Transform
the cake!" Oro was giddy with
excitement.

"But if it's gold, then we won't be
able to eat it," said Tibben, puzzled.

"Who cares!" said Oro. "It will
look so cool in gold!"

Tibben felt another shiver run
down his spine.

"Here," said Oro, handing him
a thick velvet cloak. "Put this on; it

will keep you much warmer."

"Thanks." Tibben put the velvet cloak on over the top of his plain green one. The fabric felt rich and soft. The prince was right – it was much warmer than his. He wrapped it tight around him until he couldn't see any of his old cloak at all. He looked up at the prince, smiling in the glow of the beautiful golden rug.

"OK, let's transform the cake," he said.

Chapter Six

Grandpa and Wizz returned to the Potions Shop late that night. Wizz couldn't wait to tell Tibben how she had managed to sense ants, and worms, and even Wisgar the Specs Mole! But Tibben wasn't there.

Grandpa found his note:

Hi, Grandpa and Wizz,
I'm just going out for dinner to sort something out.
I'll be back soon!
Love,
Tibben

"He's gone out," he said. "I'm sure he'll be back in the morning, little Wizz. You'll see him then."

But Wizz noticed that Grandpa's forehead had lots of lines across it. *Not happy*, Wizz told herself. *Grandpa no happy wooz.*

In the morning Grandpa looked even more worried. Tibben had still not returned.

"Wizz," he said. "You and Tibben have a special bond. I'd like you to try something. Close your eyes and try to sense him."

Wizz shut her eyes and concentrated very hard. Normally, when she was looking for something, she could feel if it was nearby. A current of energy would run from the top of her head to the tip of her tail and she would get a funny tingle inside. Today, she felt nothing. She shook her head. "No Tib Tib," she said. "Wizz no find."

"Hmm," said Grandpa. He took something out of his pocket. Wizz had never seen it before. It was round and golden. Grandpa pressed a catch and it popped open. Wizz's eyes widened.

"This is the *Master's Dial*," said Grandpa. "It's what Potions Masters use to measure Harmony and Blight."

Wizz nodded. She knew all about Harmony and Blight. Harmony was when everything felt good in the kingdom; all the creatures were happy, the waters flowed clean, the plants grew and nature thrived. Blight was a feeling of sadness and despair; the air felt heavy and misty and it seemed like nothing would go right. Wizz leaned over Grandpa's *Dial*.

The *Dial* had a little golden

arrow that pointed
up to $\mathcal{H}$ or down
to $\mathcal{B}$. Now the
arrow hovered
somewhere in
between the two,
quivering and
shaking towards Blight.

"Something's wrong," said
Grandpa, and Wizz felt a chill
inside her.

"Tib Tib!" she gasped, then
jumped up. "Wizz go," she said.
"Wizz find."

"Oh, Wizz, I should go with
you," said Grandpa, but Wizz could
see that he looked pale and tired.

"No." Wizz took the old pixie's

hand in her paw and looked into his eyes. "Wizz find," she said firmly. She picked up her Gathering Diary and a little backpack and, with a wave to Grandpa, she opened the wooden door of the Potions Shop and stepped out.

The air felt fresh and clean. *Spring is coming*, Wizz thought. She could sense the ants under the earth and smell the Scrub Nettle from a bush next to the path. She sniffed the air and turned round and round in a circle. Hmm. She caught the scent of something familiar towards the north. She walked on, sniffing as she went. Something told her that this was the right way.

Soon she came to a **Silent Bark Tree** From its hollow came a rustling sound. Wizz's ears pricked up. Someone inside was singing a low sad song. Wizz poked her head into the hollow. "Hello wooz!" she called. "All all right, right?"

There was a squeak in answer
and a louder rustle. In the darkness
Wizz could make out a Song Rabbit.
Its leg was caught in some **Bouncy
Moss**.

"Wizz help," she said softly,
and the Song Rabbit looked up at
her with big eyes. She carefully
untangled the rabbit's leg and lifted
the creature out of the hollow tree.
The rabbit blinked in the sunlight
and grinned in thanks. Wizz smiled
back. Then she had an idea – maybe
the rabbit had seen Tibben go by?

"Wizz find Tib Tib," she said.
"Where is Tib Tib?"

The Song Rabbit cocked his head
to the side, looking confused. Wizz

waved her paws in the air, as if she was pulling a cloak around her, and walked on a little way. All at  once the rabbit understood. He banged his foot and pointed north.

"That way weez?" asked Wizz.

The rabbit nodded.

"Thank wooz!" said Wizz and blew him a kiss.

Off she went, all the way to the very edge of the forest to find her best friend.

Chapter Seven

Soon Wizz came to the golden
gates of Prince Oro's palace. She
shivered. She didn't like the feel of
this place. It was cold and the air
was heavy and misty. Wizz touched
the golden gates and remembered
how Tibben had always wanted to
go inside. She ran her paw along
the gate, and at the edge she found
a thread caught on the handle.
She bent her head to sniff it –

it smelled like Tibben!

"Tib Tib!" Wizz pushed open the gate and headed up the path to the palace. She kept her head down to avoid the eyes of the huge statues on either side as she walked up to the golden door. She pushed the bell again and again but no one came. Frowning, Wizz walked round the back of the palace where she found a small courtyard.

Wizz raised her eyebrows. Lying on the ground were a golden hose, a golden broom, golden rocks and even a golden wheelbarrow! Wizz slowly turned around. She gasped as she realized that everything in the courtyard had been turned to gold!

The pebbles on the ground shone
bright yellow, the leaves of the ivy
were hard gold and Wizz picked a
pawful of berries to find that they
were now solid and cold.

She shook her head. What had
happened? Then she heard the
murmur of a familiar voice coming

from somewhere above her. "Tib Tib!" she cried. She looked up and there, at the end of the courtyard, was a tall tower.

Wizz dashed across the courtyard, slipping and sliding on the golden pebbles. At the base of the tower she searched for handholds to help her climb up, but the walls were far too high. Her eyes scanned the courtyard for anything she could use. She frowned. It was so hard to sense anything in that cold, hard place. It felt like nothing was growing; like nature had completely disappeared. Wizz shivered and shook her head to clear it.

She closed her eyes and sniffed.
She concentrated hard until she
felt a little tingle inside. Opening
her eyes, she headed straight for
a golden bush. Here the tingly
feeling was stronger. Her fur
bristled and her tail
stood on end. There
was something
special nearby!
Wizz dug
into the soil
and found a
beautiful lime-
green flower.
She lifted it to her nose and took a
deep sniff. The scent of the flower
filled her head. It smelled lush and

sweet, of thick green jungles and warm musty soil. Mmm. As she breathed it in, Wizz felt her head clear and she smiled.

She dug into the soil again and found the rest of the plant. She pulled until a long woody stem came free. It made the perfect rope! Wizz wound it round and round her paw until she had enough. Then she threw it high in the air, aiming for the top of the tower. The rope fell

straight back down. Again
and again she tried, until
her arms ached. But the
tower was just too high.
She couldn't throw the
rope-vine far enough.

Wizz sat down to think.
She leaned back against a
golden tree and closed her
eyes. Suddenly she could
sense something. What
was it? It didn't smell like
a flower or a leaf. It didn't
smell like the ants she
had sensed earlier; they
smelled like rusty metal,
but this – this smelled . . .
"Fluffy weez," said Wizz.

She lifted her head. There
was something in the tree. Wizz
jumped onto the lowest branch
and pulled herself up until she
saw a bird's nest. It was made of
sticks, but every stick had turned
golden. Wizz frowned. She
peered into the nest. Curled up
inside lay a blue Star Toucan.

"Hello wooz!" Wizz smiled.
But the bird lifted his head

weakly and dropped it again. He looked exhausted and Wizz noticed that his body was thin and frail. She looked around. From the tree she could see into the palace garden – everything was golden! All the trees, all the bushes, all the plants shone a deep yellow. There was nothing for the bird to eat!

Wizz felt around in her little backpack – she was sure she had packed some **Honey Berries** this morning. Yes! There they were.

"Eat, eat!" she said, opening her paw. The bird lifted his head and gobbled down the delicious berries. He ate and ate until he felt stronger.

"Fly, fly," said Wizz. "No good

here, wooz." She flapped her paws.
She hoped the bird understood.
He needed to find
a new nest somewhere
better. The bird chirped
at Wizz and presented
her with one of his
brightly coloured
feathers. Then he flew
down from the tree and picked up
the rope-vine in his beak.

"Yes, up, up please weez!" cried
Wizz, pointing at the tower.

The toucan nodded and flew
up to the top of the tower. Wizz
watched as he wound the rope over
and over one of the turrets.

"Thank wooz!" she called as he

shook his tail goodbye and
flew away. She smiled
and waved.

Wizz began to climb
the rope-vine. Up and
up she went, paw over
paw. She tried not
to look down at the
golden ground below.
She climbed on until
she came to a small round
window in the tower.

"Tib Tib?" she called,
then pulled herself
through the window
and into a little room.

Chapter Eight

Tibben felt tired and cold. His hands shook as he pulled Prince Oro's velvet cloak tight around him. Why couldn't he get warm? He shook his head crossly. No, he wouldn't think about that now. There was still so much to do!

Prince Oro had brought him hundreds of things to turn into gold. Tibben had transformed chairs and plates and hoses and

wheelbarrows and even plants. He
got the *Transformation Gel* right
every time now! The
prince had told him
he was amazing.
He was making
Oro so happy!
Tibben
looked at the
prince, sitting
on a golden
cushion, Padge
curled up next to him. The prince
was stroking the Lightning Pup's
soft purple fur.

"Hey," the prince drawled lazily.
"Let's turn Padge's tail golden!
Then it will match his collar!"

Tibben lifted his **Mage Nut** bowl and started on another batch of *Transformation Gel*. Just as he was adding the Chrysalis Powder he heard a squeaky voice.

"Tib Tib!" it said. Tibben frowned. That voice was familiar. Then he saw a bundle of fluffy white fur come flying towards him and leap into his arms.

"Wizz!" he cried. "What are you doing here?"

"Home wooz," said Wizz, tugging his hand with her paw.

"Sorry, Wizz," said Tibben. "I've got too much to do. You go ahead. I'll come later."

Wizz shook her head and

stamped her foot. "Come, come!" she said.

"No," Tibben turned away from Wizz and stirred his potion. Wizz jumped up onto the table and pulled his **Mage Nut** bowl away.

"Hey!" shouted Tibben. "I need that!" He yanked it back.

"Home!" Wizz insisted.

"No!"

Wizz looked deep into Tibben's eyes. "Grandpa wooz," she said softly.

For a second Tibben thought about Grandpa waiting in the warm, cosy little wooden shop, with a cup of Hazelwood tea and a hug for Tibben. Then the sparkle of a golden plate caught his eye.

"No," he said. He had to keep working.

But every time he tried to concentrate on the transformation, Wizz darted around, jumping onto his shoulders or touching his hand with her paw.

"Stop it, Wizz!" Tibben shouted. "I'm busy!"

Wizz stopped. Then she pulled a bright, lime-green flower out of her backpack. She held it right up to Tibben's face so he had no choice but to breathe the scent in. He took a sniff. Mmm. It smelled warm and soft; of wet earth and lush jungle. A well of happiness bubbled up inside Tibben. All at once he longed to be outside in the fresh air, touching the plants and rolling in the grass. Tibben stood up straighter. He flung off Prince Oro's velvet cloak and smoothed out his own plain green one. He rubbed the fabric in between his fingers and ran his fingers over his **Glints**. They made a little humming noise and Tibben smiled.

"Wizz!" he cried. "What am I doing here? I don't know why I wanted to make all this gold!"

Padge gave a happy woof from the sofa – Tibben's hands flew to his mouth in horror.

"Oh, Wizz," he cried. "I nearly turned poor Padge's tail golden." His eyes filled with tears. "I should have helped the prince, but I haven't. I've made things worse. Please, may I use that flower?"

Tibben rushed to Oro's side. He held up the flower and the prince sniffed at it. Slowly Oro sat up.

He blinked and rubbed his eyes.

"Prince Oro, we have to stop," said Tibben.

At first the prince shook his head.

"Oro," said Tibben gently. "Everything is golden. We haven't eaten for hours because all the food is golden; all the cake and all the chocolates. The dancers can't dance because the golden floor is too slippery. Your bed is hard and uncomfortable; all the carpets are cold – and look at Padge – look at his beautiful fur and wagging tail. We can't turn him golden!"

Oro breathed in slowly. He stroked his faithful puppy, burying his fingers deep into his fur.

"I'm sorry, my friend," he whispered to Padge. Then, looking up at Tibben, he said, "Yes, let's stop!"

Tibben moved to the window and leaned out to look at the golden garden below him.

"Wizz, this is all my fault. I have to fix it."

Chapter Nine

Tibben opened *The Book of Potions*. He turned page after page until he came to:

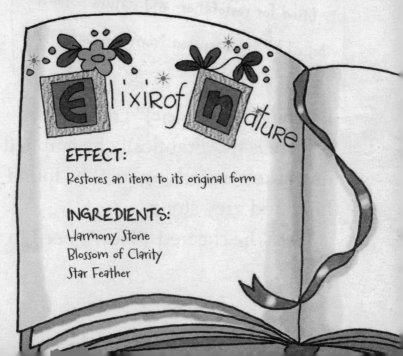

EFFECT:
Restores an item to its original form

INGREDIENTS:
Harmony Stone
Blossom of Clarity
Star Feather

"Harmony Stone?" Tibben was puzzled. "What's a Harmony Stone?"

Wizz shrugged.

"Hmm," said Tibben. He turned to the back of *The Book of Potions* to look in the glossary.

Harmony Stone

Used for restoration and nature potions.

Must be transformed from a Mage Stone.

"The Mage Stone!" cried Tibben. "Where is it?" Frantically he emptied his pockets, searching until he found the round grey stone.

"Yes!" he cheered. "Now I need to

transform it into a Harmony Stone."
He reached for his **Mage Nut**
bowl and took the last spoonful of
Transformation Gel. As he painted
the gel onto the stone, he took a
deep breath and focused hard on
Harmony. Tibben thought about the
green plants and flowers, about the
rocks and soil, about all the different
creatures in the kingdom, with their
wings and claws and horns and
fangs and feathers and fur. He smiled
as the warm feeling of Harmony
spread through his body. Everything
was right again.

Tibben looked down. The grey
Mage Stone was a deep brown now,
shiny and warm all over.

"I think it's worked!" he said. "Wizz, we have a Harmony Stone!"

"Woozoo!" cried Wizz.

Tibben turned back to look at the recipe. He read through the rest of the ingredients.

"Blossom of Clarity?" He looked at Wizz. She pointed to the lime-green flower in his hand and he smiled.

"What about Star Feather?" he asked. From her backpack Wizz pulled out the bright blue feather given to her by the toucan.

"Wizz!" laughed Tibben. "You are amazing! Prince Oro – look. Wizz might not be a Potions Master but she is the most talented Gatherer there has ever been," he said proudly, "and she's my best friend." He hugged her tight. "I'm sorry," he whispered.

Wizz hugged him back, her fluffy warm paws soft around his neck.

"Let's turn everything back to normal," he said.

Tibben squeezed the juice from the Blossom of Clarity and pulled off the fluffiest bits of the Star Feather.

Then he added his freshly made Harmony Stone and stirred. Prince Oro and Wizz leaned over the bowl and watched as the Harmony Stone dissolved and the mixture became a thin brown liquid.

"Here we go," said Tibben, and he moved around the room, flicking the liquid onto each golden object one by one. Slowly they started to change. The golden chairs turned back to wood, the cushion became plump and soft, the plates returned to white china and the cake was soon delicious once again.

"Thank you," said Prince Oro in a serious voice. "I think that's the best potion you've ever made."

Tibben hugged him.

"Hey!" said the prince. "What's that?" He pointed to Tibben's cloak.

Tibben looked down, and there, before his eyes, was a **Glint**! A **Ruby** level **Glint**! He grinned at Wizz. "Come on," he said. "Let's go home."

Chapter Ten

It took a while for Tibben and Wizz to get out of the palace. Tibben wanted to restore everything he had transformed so that nothing was left golden.

Finally it was done. At the gates they waved goodbye to Prince Oro.

"Come and visit me again," he said. "I'd be honoured to have you anytime – both of you." He bowed to Wizz and Wizz bowed in return.

Back through Steadysong Forest they walked. Tibben couldn't get enough of the plants and flowers. He sniffed every petal and touched every leaf. He was rubbing the bark of a tree when he heard the rumbling call of a Star Toucan. He looked up to find a bird waving at Wizz from a nest.

"Is he a friend of yours?" asked

Tibben. Wizz nodded and waved back. "He looks very happy." Wizz smiled.

Tibben looked at her. *What has she been up to?* he wondered. He was even more puzzled when, as they passed a Song Rabbit singing a happy tune, the rabbit hopped straight up to Wizz and shook her paw.

Tibben stopped. "Wizz, I don't know what you've been doing, but it looks like you've been trying to help creatures, while I've just been making things worse. This Glint should be for you, not me," he said miserably.

Wizz climbed up his legs to put her furry arms around his neck. "Tib Tib fix Blight," she said.

"Only with your help," he said. "Oh, Wizz, I promise I won't leave

you out ever again. We're a team, you and I, and we should stay together."

Wizz nuzzled into his neck. "Team wooz," she said, and Tibben carried her all the way back to the Potions Shop.

"Aha!" said Grandpa. "I see you found him, Wizz!"

"Thank goodness she did," said Tibben. "I'm sorry, Grandpa. I haven't been a very good potions maker."

Grandpa put his arm around Tibben. "Things don't always go right," he said, "but the important thing is that you found a way to help in the end. And look . . ."

He pulled out the *Master's Dial* and showed Tibben the arrow firmly pointing towards Harmony.

Tibben smiled. "I'm so glad," he said. "And I got a Glint too!" He showed off the **Ruby Glint**.

"Well done!" said Grandpa.

"It's strange," Tibben said. "I thought I would get a Glint the first time I managed to transform something, but I didn't get one when I made the rug gold."

"Do you know why?" asked Grandpa.

"I think so." Tibben nodded. "It's because I didn't make the potion to help someone, isn't it? I didn't bring Harmony back."

"That's right, my boy," said Grandpa as he ruffled Tibben's hair. "Being a Potions Master is not just about being able to make a potion. It's about making the right potion; the potion that helps."

Tibben nodded.

Grandpa squeezed his shoulder. "Come on, let's all go inside and have some Hazelwood tea."

"I'll make it," said Tibben, "while Wizz shows you her Gathering Diary. She's amazing," he said proudly.

Grandpa grinned. "You both are," he replied.

Potions

Extracts from *The Book of Potions:*

Clean-up Powder
Effect: Makes anything sparkly clean
Ingredients:
- Soap Vine
- Devil's Shine
- Scrub Nettle

Disappearing Potion
Effect: Makes anything or anyone disappear for two hours
Ingredients:
- Chameleon Claw
- Silent Bark
- Glass Pearl

Elixir of Nature
Effect: Restores an item to its original form
Ingredients:
- Harmony Stone
- Blossom of Clarity
- Star Feather

Flying Potion

Effect: Allows flight of up to 30 metres, for a period of 15 minutes

Ingredients:
- Cloud Lotus
- Light Puff
- Golden Root

Invisible Potion

Effect: Makes anything invisible for three hours

Ingredients:
- Chameleon Claw
- Glass Pearl
- Silent Bark

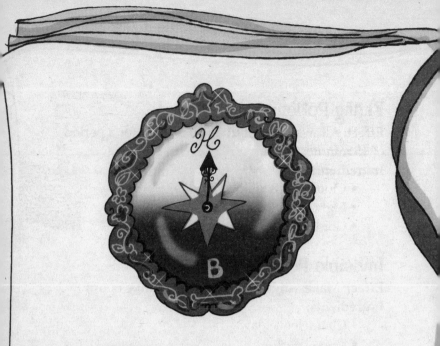

Iron Cream
Effect: Repairs and toughens shell, horn and bone
Ingredients:

- Strong Scale
- Pearly Shell
- Dwarfsteel

Sticking Potion
Effect: Sticks anything to anything
Ingredients:

- Gumspider Web
- Red Clay
- Troll Slime

Transformation Gel

Effect: Transforms any object

Ingredients:

- Chameleon Claw
- Chrysalis Powder
- Glass Flower

Waterskate Powder

Effect: Allows the drinker to walk and skate on water

Ingredients:

- Steady Leaf
- Light Puff
- Cloud Lotus

Ingredients

Extracts from
The Glossary of Magic Ingredients

Blossom of Clarity
Rare lime-green flower found in the grounds of palaces.
Used in **Elixir of Nature** and **Jungle Potion**

Bouncy Moss
Grows in Moonlight Meadow and Steadysong Forest.
Look for green curled springs. Used for **Jumping Potion**

Chameleon Claw
Exchange with Rainbow Chameleons on Blue Mountain
after a favour is performed. Used for **Invisible Potion**,
Transformation Gel and **Camouflage Potion**

Chrysalis Powder
Made from ground-up abandoned butterfly houses
in Moonlight Meadow. Used in **Beauty Potion** and
Handsome Cream as well as **Transformation Gel**

Cloud Lotus
Floats on Lake Sapphire. White fluffy plant. Key ingredient
in **Flying** and **Floating Potions** as well as **Dreaming
Potions**, **Hover Potion**, **Rooting Potion**, **Waterskate
Powder** and **Rain Potion**

Devil's Shine
Bright shining plant – requires podding. Grows in Western Valley for **Clean-up Powder**

Dwarfsteel
Exchange with Ice Dwarfs in the Frozen Tundra. Used for **Magic Rope** and **Iron Cream**

Fast Lotus
Found on edge of the Green Silk Grasses. Thin, sharp plant always covered in Racing Snails. Used for all **Speed Potions**, **Ten Legs Potion**, **High Reach Potion** and **Arm Stretch Cream**

Glass Flower
Rare ingredient found in Steadysong Forest. Used in **Beauty Potion**, **Handsome Cream** and **Transformation Gel**

Glass Pearl
Dive for these in Lake Sapphire. Found in transparent oysters. Key ingredient in **Invisible Potion**, **Disappearing Potion** and **Camouflage Potion**

Golden Root
Grows underground in Moonlight Meadow. Look for golden flower and dig under left side. Used for **Flying Potion**, **Floating Potion**, **Hover Potion** and **Rooting Potion**. Store underground

Gumspider Web

Found in Steadysong Forest. Take one strand at a time only.
Used for **Sticking Potion, Climbing Potion** and **Tidy Thread**

Harmony Stone

Used for restoration and nature
potions. Must be transformed
from a **Mage Stone**

Honey Berries

Edible berries. Grows in the
Tangled Glade. Used to make **Elixir of Moon Pearl**

Light Puff

Comes from the breath of a dragon. Used in all **Flying Potions,
Hover Potions, Rooting Potion** and **Sweet Tune Potion**

Mage Stone

Smooth grey stone. Found underneath the Mage Nut tree. Used
to test potions. Can be transformed into a **Harmony Stone**

Pearly Shell

Found inside salt-water clamshells, deep in the Fickle Ocean.
Used for **Iron Cream**

Red Clay

Found at the bottom of Lake Sapphire and Bubble River. Used
for **Sticking Potion**

Scrub Nettle

Grows in Steadysong Forest. Beware of its sting. Used for
Clean-up Powder

Silent Bark

Peeled from the hollow Silent Bark Tree in Steadysong Forest.
Key ingredient in **Invisible Potion, Disappearing Potion**
and **Camouflage Potion**

Soap Vine

Grows on Troll Hills – a distinctive foaming green plant. Used
for **Clean-up Powder**

Spider Grass

Rare curly black plant found in Steadysong Forest. Used for
Drawing Potion

Star Feather

Exchange with Star Toucans. Bright blue feather. Used in **Elixir
of Nature**

Steady Leaf

Found in Steadysong Forest. Used for **Balance Potion,
Waterskate Powder** and **Singsong Potion**

Strong Scale

Exchange with fish in the Fickle Ocean for **Swim Fast Gel.**
Used for **Iron Cream**

Troll Slime

Grows under bridges in Troll Hills. Used for **Sticking Potion,
Climbing Potion** and **Tidy Thread**

Wizz's Quiz

Test your knowledge – how many questions can you answer?

1. Where can you find **Chrysalis Powder**?

2. At the start of Tibben's journey, which two Glints does he need before he can take the Master's Challenge?

3. What new animal does Tibben create when he first tries to make *Transformation Gel*?

4. What is Padge's job?

5. What are the missing words in this description?

   When Tibben arrived at the palace, Prince Oro was wearing "a _ _ _ _ _ _ dressing gown and sparkly _ _ _ shoes that _ _ _ _ _ _ up at the toes".

6. What does Grandpa use to measure Harmony and Blight?
7. In which tree does Wizz find the Song Rabbit?
8. What colour is Blossom of Clarity?

Turn to the back of the book for the solution to this puzzle!

Potion Scramble

The names of these potions ingredients are missing some letters! Can you help Tibben by filling in the blanks?

1. T_O_L _L_M_

2. _H_Y_A_I_ P_W_E_

3. H_R_O_YS_O_E

4. D_A_F_T_E_

5. C_A_E_N C_A_

Turn to the back of the book for the solution to this puzzle!

Crossword

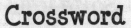

Solve the riddles below to find
the characters in this crossword!

	1.						
2.				3.			
		4.					
	5.						

Across

2. I am an ancient Potions Master. I have to retire;
   won't Tibben learn faster?
5. I'm busy learning all kinds of potions:
   ointments, powders, gels and lotions!

Down

1. I live in a palace. I'm the son of a king. And I love gold
   more than anything.
3. Lightning fast and still only a pup. If you've a message
   to send, then look me up!
4. I gather plants for the Potions Shop. Dashing around,
   I never stop!

Turn to the back of the book for the solution to this puzzle!

Solutions

Wizz's Quiz

1. In abandoned butterfly houses in Moonlight Meadow
2. Ruby and Diamond
3. A Teacup Spider!
4. He's a Lightning Pup – one of Prince Oro's messengers
5. velvet; red; curled
6. The Master's Dial
7. A Silent Bark Tree
8. Lime-green

Potion Scramble

1. Troll Slime
2. Chrysalis Powder
3. Harmony Stone
4. Dwarfsteel
5. Chameleon Claw

Crossword

	1. O							
2. G	R	A	N	D	3. P	A		
	O				A			
					D			
		4. W			G			
	5. T	I	B	B	E	N		
		Z						
		Z						